BLUE COLLAR NECROMANCY

STEFON MEARS

Also by Stefon Mears

The Rise of Magic Series
Magician's Choice
Sleight of Mind
Lunar Alchemy
Three Fae Monte
The Sphinx Principle
Double Backed Magic
Mercury Fold (forthcoming)

Cavan Oltblood Series
Half a Wizard
The Ice Dagger
Spells of Undeath
The Shaman's Eye (forthcoming)

Power City Tales
Not Quite Bulletproof
No Money in Heroism

Standalones
Blue Collar Necromancy
The Mosh Pit from Hell
The Hireling
The Captain's Cat
Save Whiskers!
The Ogre of Threepeaks
Between the Cracks
Sects and the City
Prince of a Thousand Worlds
Devil's Night
Portal-Land, Oregon
Stealing from Pirates
Fade to Gold
With a Broken Sword
Twice Against the Dragon
The House on Cedar Street
Sudden Death
On the Edge of Faerie

Short Story Collections
Spell Slingers
Twisted Timelines
Longhairs and Short Tales: A Collection of Cat Stories
Dangerous Space
Confronting Legends (Spells & Swords Vol. 1)
The Patreon Collection, Vol. 1-8 (Vol. 9, coming soon)

Spells for Hire Series
Devil's Shoestring
Zombie Powder
Spirit Trap
Dragon's Blood

The Telepath Trilogy
Surviving Telepathy
Immoral Telepathy
Targeting Telepathy

Edge of Humanity Series
Caught Between Monsters
Hunting Monsters

Jumpstart Duchy Series
Into the Torn Kingdoms
The Dragon's Gold
The Gift Castle
The Deadly Feast
The King's Test
Triumph in the Torn Kingdoms

Nonfiction
The 30-Day Novel and Beyond!

Published by Thousand Faces Publishing, Portland, Oregon

http://1kfaces.com

ISBN: 978-1-948490-54-2

BLUE COLLAR NECROMANCY

Was supposed to be a bright day, but it wasn't. Storm clouds came rolling over Portland from the west like tourists hell-bent on seeing everything *now*. Rain hadn't hit yet, but the winds whistled their warnings.

In one way, I admit, I didn't mind. October shouldn't've felt as warm as it had over the last week. Portland has seasons, and fall should feel like fall.

Still. On this day I would've preferred good weather. For once this job was finished. Knew I'd feel better coming back outside if blue skies and singing birds greeted me.

I know, I know. I've been in necromantic repairs and services professionally for two years. I ought to be over that whole creepy, working-with-the-dead sensation by now. But I'm not.

The other guys down at the station, I know they're laughing at me behind my back for it. But I can't help it.

Every problem I get called out for has to do with some aspect of a dead *person*. Someone – or a piece of someone – that hasn't moved on to what comes next. That got *stuck*. And that thought, yeah, it creeps me out and sometimes wakes me up at night.

Oh, and *no*. I don't fucking know what comes next. The dead I deal with are *here*. Far as I know, at the end of a job they got an equal shot at either heaven, hell, oblivion or some other option from one of the many, *many* belief systems running around this world.

None of my business where they *go*. But they can't stay *here*.

Anyway, those cold winds were blowing when I got out of the van. And since it wasn't raining, I wasn't allowed to wear a jacket over the black cotton jumpsuit.

Mark of the trade, after all. And our trade isn't colorful, like the elementalists. Least black is slimming, 'cause this job makes me indulge in my comfort snacks more than my waistline likes.

So the wind was making me shiver, which is never a good look in my line of work. Could make someone think I'm afraid of what I'm about to do, which is ridiculous. So I hauled out my pack and slung it over one shoulder. Casual as I could be. Black nylon, that pack, and it carried all my tools of the trade, organized nice and neat.

I gave the back of the van a once over, making sure I'd reloaded it properly before taking it out this morning. Didn't want to go back to the station for extra reagents or any of the bigger equipment, if I needed something. But the layout in the back of the van looked good, so I slammed the door closed and double-checked the address.

2323 Mockingbird Court. Honestly, though, I could've guessed this house without checking the work order. Looked too gothic for the neighborhood. Everything else around me was part of some kind of cookie-cutter housing development in the '90s, but this one here, at the top of this little hill in southwest Portland, didn't match. Probably the oldest house on the block, and probably once inhabited by the family that owned all the land around it, before that land started getting parceled out and sold off.

The house reminded me of a teenager who grew eight inches over the summer. Stretched upward and too skinny, like it should be teetering. The shingled roof looked old. Not just weathered, but beaten down. Like depression had settled in. And that roof peaked in more places than most houses should.

Weird angles. Weird, skinny windows.

Should've gone the rest of the way and painted the house black. Complete the raven image it seemed to project. But no, they'd painted it a dark blue.

Still. All that might've been weird, but it wasn't *wyrd*. In the older sense. The important sense.

But one thing about this house, what I could see of it from the street, did strike me as possibly wyrd. Whole yard was Oregon native plants. Ferns and rhododendrons and grapes and roses, all the local variety. Common practice, of course. But in this case, none of them grew within ... maybe fifteen feet of the house itself. Not even the Corsican mint they used as ground cover. And I wouldn't have believed a fiery moat could hold back mint.

All the smells were normal. For the plants, I mean, though the street's old asphalt carried its usual smells too. I suppose. Point is, I could've been walking up limestone stepping stones on the way through anyone's garden, given the smells.

Those stepping stones continued across the bare dirt to front steps so worn out they sagged in the middle.

Thirteen of those stairs, by the way, which I thought was a little on-the-nose for a place like this one.

Front porch had a pair of old wicker rocking chairs, and already I was expecting those things to start rocking. Just to mock me.

But no. So far, everything was quiet and ... normal.

I didn't trust it one bit.

I avoided the saggy middles as I made my way up those stairs. I know a tripping hazard when I see one.

Porch itself didn't sag, which was encouraging. Last thing I needed was to end up in a house so weak it shifted with my weight. And I'm not all that big a guy.

Porch was well-swept, too. Good sign, there. If they showed this much care for the interior, it would affect all of the spirits of the house. The ones they wanted there, not just the one – or ones – I'd been called out to get rid of.

Knocker looked like a gargoyles face, with the grin holding the ring. I didn't use it. Looked too much like a potential token to me, and I wasn't technically on their dime yet. Instead I pounded on the heavy hardwood door.

Door's seal wasn't perfect. I could hear voices on the other side. No details, but enough to pick out two of them.

Finally the door opened. Two women stood there. The one holding the door was younger – thirtysomething, redheaded, in jeans and a dark blue sweater. The other woman stood just behind her. Thinner. Maybe twice as old, but still some red in her graying hair. Black dress, black sweater.

Sounds weird, I know, but I had to pay attention to things like clothes for a job like this. See, one of the problems that creeps up are the amateurs trying to play wizard. They call up something they can't put back down, you know? And usually they're wearing little amulets or talismans as necklaces or earrings.

Or wearing all black. So I had one suspicion before I even knew what was going on.

I tabled that for now, though.

"Morning," I said. "I'm Ollie, your magitech from Curwin Necro-mantic. I believe you're expecting me?"

The younger woman scrutinized my face, then my jumpsuit and nylon bag. "Last name?"

I smiled at that. Caution was a good watchword, when it came to dealing with magic-users. "Jefferson."

Wasn't my real name, of course, for my own protection from the various forces we dealt with in work. It was my working name. Much the way that the old occult orders used to give their initiates special names, pretty much every magitech in any of the branches went by a working name.

A lot of working names had deep meaning. I liked that mine came off kind of bland, and harder to remember.

"That's him then, Connie," the older woman said. "Let him in already."

"Not yet," the younger one – Connie, apparently – said. "What time did I place the call to schedule this service?'

"You called yesterday afternoon, at three thirty-three p.m. Your call was taken by Dwayne, who told you this was the first available appointment, and identified me as the magitech."

She nodded. "Please, come in to provide your service and nothing else."

"You haven't formally told me the service," I said. "But I can agree to come inside, listen to your problem, come to agreement about the service and expected needs and costs, and perform no other tasks but those and any related to the job we agree on."

Connie considered that for a moment.

"For whatever it's worth," I said, "I applaud your caution, and assure you that what I've just said is standard phrasing. I can show it to you in our manual, if you like."

"That won't be necessary," she said. "Under those terms and those terms only, I invite you in until such time as whatever service we agree to is complete."

I chuckled. "You've studied."

"Family tradition."

She stepped aside then, and I entered that strange, gothic house.

***

I HALF-EXPECTED TO BE LED INTO A KITCHEN. FOR SOME REASON, THESE discussions almost always seem to take place in kitchens. Perhaps because kitchens form the metaphorical heart of most houses. Everything revolves around them, one way or another, except in the case of those families who honestly never cook, or really keep much food in the house. The kind who order everything delivered.

Instead, they led me to a dining room, and along the way I got my first look at the layout of the house.

Cramped. And stuffed. This house had clearly been in someone's family for generations, and no one ever threw anything away. The wood-paneled walls were covered in small paintings and photographs, some of which looked to have been quite recent, while others might've gone back more than a century.

And then there was the bric-a-brac. The already cramped hall had runner tables, covered in all sorts of odds and ends.

Oh, you unkind gods that rule matters of life, death and beyond. Damn near *anything* in this house might be a token. I was literally surrounded by hundreds of things that might've been decades old. That might've been favorite possessions of important family members before they died, and have some small part of those family members still clinging...

I resolved not to open myself to any of the deeper perceptions until it was absolutely necessary, and then only as much as I absolutely had to.

This whole house could've been one big nightmare.

Or it could've just been a house full of stuff. Technically, that was a possibility.

But given my luck, I knew which way I was betting.

Especially given that I could smell dust. Oh, not a ton. They – or someone – clearly did domestic tasks around here. It was just that, overstuffed as this house was, getting *all* that dust and keeping it from accumulating faster than it was cleaned was just too much to ask of anyone.

For whatever good it might do me, I did notice that I could smell some kind of lemon oil, as well. Probably used to clean the ancient hardwood floors. Which might've been old and scuffed, but looked to otherwise be in good shape.

I didn't smell cats, but I expected to. This just seemed like the kind of place where a half-dozen cats of various ages poked around, ready to jump out at me when I least needed it.

I love cats. But their sense of humor sometimes doesn't sit well with me while I'm working.

We followed that hall through a good portion of the house – passing only closed doors, which had to have been deliberate. And overcautious. I mean, yeah, you don't generally want magic workers knowing more about you, personally, than you have to. Just in case. But this was going to an extreme that bordered on insulting.

Nevertheless, I kept my working smile on my face and followed them into a dining room that...

Maybe I'd misjudged the house's width? Because the entry to the dining room was about as far down as I'd expect. And given that the hall we'd been following seemed to bisect the bottom floor, there shouldn't have been more than fifteen feet of house to my left. Twenty at the most.

Yet the hall ended in two doors, with the one on the left leading into the dining room. Nice, high ceiling, warm wood paneling, fireplace (cold at the moment, but woodburning), fancy breakfront full of antiques.

And the dining table – which I'd expected to sit parallel to the hall I'd just left, was perpendicular instead. The room was wider than it was long. Had to be thirty feet wide. Easily

I'll admit. I itched to open one of my deeper senses a little early and see if this was more than just a trick of good architecture. But I was resolved not to do so until I was on the job, and trying to solve these people's problem.

Technically I could have opened those senses, by the way, without breaking my word. I could argue that understanding the possibly strange magics of a room I was expected to occupy would be a fair action as part of coming inside and listening to their problem. Especially since, if there were any issues in those spells, the room could present a potential hazard to my person.

Entirely unlikely, of course. Not as casual as these two were about their dining room. But it was a loophole, if I felt the need to exploit it.

They both took seats at what had to be the biggest honking dining table I'd ever seen in real life. Easily a dozen feet long and eight feet wide. Looked like it had been ornately carved from teak by someone who had entirely too much teak to work with and too much time on their hands.

Hell, even pulling out my own chair to sit down took effort. Whuf.

I took a seat at one end of the table. The older woman at the other end, with Connie – if that was her name, and not a nickname for my benefit – to her right.

"All right," I said. "What problem has led you to call for me?"

"Our heater has failed," Connie said, apparently leading the conversation on their end, while the older woman watched attentively.

"You called the wrong service then," I said, shaking my head. "By agreement of the guilds – and for obvious reasons – all heating systems are handled by elementalists. I'm not even allowed to touch a heating system."

"We've already had an elementalist out here," the older woman said. "Two days ago. According to his report, our salamanders were driven out by remnants."

"And *he* says," Connie said with no little irritation in her voice, "that *he* can't fix it until someone in *your* line of work handles the remnants first."

I nodded. "That's a different matter. Though I'll need to see his report certifying the situation."

Apparently that wasn't a dark blue placemat at Connie's place at the table. It was a file folder. She pulled out some papers and slid them down the table toward me. I had to get up and fetch them the rest of the way myself, but it seemed petty to quibble about that.

I scanned the papers as I resumed my seat. As I went over them, the older woman said, "Quite an arrangement you guilds have. Multiple calls for different services, all to handle one problem."

"But it's not one problem," I said absently, making sure his report agreed with what they'd told me. "It's two problems. The elementals and the remnants. And believe me, no one can handle both for a very good reason."

"Which is?"

I smiled at them both. "Whatever tradition your family has, clearly it does not include those things we consider trade secrets, or you'd already know the answer. But everything appears to be in order. Just let me make a copy for our records."

I dug a file folder of blank pages out of my nylon bag. Three pages in the elementalist's report, so I withdrew three sheets and set them beside that report. I reached under my right sleeve for my Curwin Necromantic bracelet.

We deal mainly in remnants and such, but every magical profession has plenty of uses for servitors. Those artificial sorts of spirits we constructed to handle specific tasks.

This obsidian bracelet with its six garnets housed six such servitors, and I activated the one that made copies.

In short order, the blanks were perfect duplicates of the elementalist's report.

Then it was just a matter of brief discussion about fees, repair time and so forth, and I could actually get started on this gig.

NATURALLY, I FOUND THE FURNACE IN THE CREEPIEST BASEMENT IT HAD ever been my displeasure to enter. It sat at the bottom of a long set of limestone stairs. Dark red limestone. And lit, of course, only by a single bare bulb whose luminosity would make a solitary taper candle look like a bonfire.

The walls were that same dark red limestone, and all this limestone got me thinking.

Despite sitting on the Ring of Fire, Portland still believed in basements. Most houses had one. And while most of them were dug out of dirt, some did, indeed, have to get cut out of rock. But that rock was usually some variety of basalt.

Limestone, that was odd. Which made me wonder if this house was, in fact, built on a limestone foundation, or if, rather, the foundation was dirt. And all this limestone had been *installed.*

If so, why limestone? I couldn't believe it was for the look. After all, why pay that much money for the look, and barely light it?

I paused on the stairs – shivering again, because it was colder down here, though still a natural enough kind of cold – and knocked on the walls.

Couldn't tell much. But I got the impression that the limestone used for the walls here was much thicker than tiles.

Just something to file away for now. In case it became important.

Twenty-six stairs down.

At the bottom of the stairs was a limestone room, vaguely lit by a bulb that wasn't working any harder than the one at the top of the stairs.

The room was pentagonal, with a single door in the exact center of each wall. The doors were also painted dark red, to match the limestone. Like the whole room had been coated in dried blood. A heart with five valves.

That wasn't the creepy part though. Or rather, not the creepi*est* part.

The walls were covered in shelves. And the shelves were covered in taxidermy. Thirteen housecats, of various breeds, and seven dogs, all of them black Labrador retrievers.

Like a museum of dead family pets. Or at least, that's what I hoped they'd been. That they'd been happy animals, living long lives knowing only love and joy, and commemorated after natural deaths by owners who couldn't quite bring themselves to say goodbye.

But honestly, even if that was the exact case, I still thought it was creepy as hell. But then, I didn't have to live here.

I did have to be down here, though. Because this was where the furnace was. My starting point. Possibly my ending point too. If everything just happened to go my way today.

Hope springs eternal in the mind of the necromancer.

The furnace was an upright box just off the stairs. Maybe four feet high and two feet wide, sitting flush against the wall. Made of almond wood, and painted a bright orange, with a single red triangle, one point up.

"Against the wall?" I grumbled. "Why did they have to put it against the wall? Touching the floor would be more than good enough. Or the ceiling. But no. Probably thought they were putting it out of the way. And all *their* work is contained, isn't it? No consideration for the possibility of another guild having to touch their precious..."

I let my grumbling go then through another sigh, and looked anew at the furnace.

Concept was simple enough. I had a pretty good idea of how it worked, even though my own skills at elemental magic weren't quite good enough to qualify as a journeyman. Not unless I dedicated maybe six months of practice to it.

Anyway, I knew they built the box to house the salamanders. Those spirits of fire that would heat the house. Might only be one of those, might be one per floor, or some other arrangement, depending on the needs and budget of the homeowners.

All of the fire spirits' bindings and core instructions would be written inside, on the wood itself, in the custom language their guild used. Yadda yadda yadda.

Probably a very elegant system. When it was working. Which, even without opening to the deeper perceptions, I could tell it wasn't. I'd know that even if I hadn't been sent down here to help solve the issue.

The room was cold.

Well, with the box against the wall – and I do mean *flush*. I doubt I could've gotten a business card between that furnace and the wall – I couldn't easily encircle it. And without a consulting elementalist on hand, I couldn't just *move* the box to someplace more convenient for me. Not without violating the agreement between our guilds, and I wasn't going to do that. Not without a *very* good reason. And a call to my superiors. And possibly to my guild rep.

Just meant my job would be harder.

I looked over the almond wood box with a sigh. Couldn't move it. Couldn't open it. Couldn't even take a shaving of the wood for a link, because that would be *damaging* the box, which was also a no-no.

Working with this box could become a serious pain in my ass.

All right. What did I know for certain, despite the caginess of Connie and the older woman?

I knew this house had an elemental-based heating system. I knew that system housed its elementals in this box. I knew that those elementals were absent. And I had been told that the elementals had been "driven out" by "remnants."

Hmm. Two terms that – in my mind, not the elementalist's – required quotes there. Which meant two areas of uncertainty at this stage.

I'd take them one at a time.

Now, "driven out" could mean a lot of things. Could mean they were sent back to whatever plane of existence they came from in the first place. Could mean they'd had their bonds broken, and run amuck someplace. Could mean...

Could mean a few different options here.

I pulled out my copy of the elementalist's report and went over it again. Last time, I'd only checked enough to make sure that it was both legitimate and expressly included permission for my guild to investigate the matter.

In the middle of page two, I found my answer. And I didn't like it.

This house's furnace had once contained three, c-grade salamanders. Which was pretty darned impressive for a personal residence. I mean, the a- and b-grade types were restricted to military use only. C-grade required special permits to use privately.

And the owners here had wanted *three* of them.

That meant that the furnace had divided the house's needs in three ways, one covered by each salamander. Since the water was piped and not elemental – even stranger, given the money they'd invested in their heating system – one of them probably handled heating and cooling the water. Extravagant, but it could be quick and precise for more than a dozen simultaneous uses of water.

Another c-grade salamander could easily handle heating or cooling every room of the house to different desired temperatures. Even taking heat from one room and giving it to another.

But what did they need a third for? I mean, either of the first two could've handled all these duties for a building three, maybe five times the size of this house.

I didn't strictly need to know what they wanted with these salamanders, though. At least, not at this point.

No, I had enough to worry about with what I'd learned in the middle of page two of that report.

See, in my mind, "remnant" had been in quotes because in much the same way I'm not qualified to work professionally with elementals, elementalists aren't qualified to work professionally with the dead. And the fact that an elementalist *claimed* a remnant had caused the problem, didn't mean they were right.

But on the middle of page two of that report, I found out what had happened to those three, c-grade elementals.

Their binding spells had been *broken*. Without any of the physical representations being damaged in the slightest. Now, in most cases, I would write that off as face-saving phrasing to cover for someone who didn't get the initial bindings right.

But if that were the case, those salamanders would've been around here somewhere, causing trouble. The elementalist called in would've had to catch them and force them into temporary housing until the furnace could be fixed. That would be reflected in his report and his bill.

But those elementals were gone. And it was the professional opinion of the consulting elementalist – a *master* elementalist, I should note – that those salamanders had been *stolen*. That whoever or whatever had broken their bindings had rebound them and sent them off to do something else.

A thought that sent a chill down my spine.

The elementalist had been right about this much. The living couldn't do that. Not without at least *tampering* with the physical portions of the bindings.

Only a spirit could do that. Which meant either a daemon – industry term for such things as demons, angels, fae, djinn, ghuls and so on which are all quite different from each other, but needed a catch-all category to differentiate them from the other primary categories – an elemental, a servitor, or the dead.

The consulting elementalist had ruled out elementals, and he should know.

Couldn't be a servitor, because if servitors could be designed to pull that off, what we have of a magical infrastructure would collapse.

Couldn't be a daemon, because everything in that catch-all category left an energetic signature a mile wide. Wouldn't even need to open to the deeper perceptions to spot that influence.

Which meant it had to be the dead. Which was why the elementalist assumed it was a remnant.

But he was wrong. A mere remnant couldn't overcome a binding.

No. I was dealing with something much, much more dangerous.

I was dealing with a revenant.

NOW, A REMNANT, THAT'S JUST A LITTLE BIT OF SOMEONE THAT GETS left behind for one reason or another. Might be the way a person dies. Sudden deaths, especially violent ones with some kind of emotion involved, are the most common. They lead to those things that most people think of as "hauntings."

You know. Cold spots. Odd noises. Half-formed specters moaning or speaking or just turning and walking through the wall. That kind of thing.

Other times, remnants are the result of someone being ... well ... let's say *excessively attached* to a place or an object (or sometimes even a person) and leaving a little of themselves behind, to look after what they loved so well. Like Grampa's favorite muscle car that "has a mind of its own" once in a while. Or maybe has a few quirks, or a lot of "personality."

Yeah. A lot of those go unnoticed or aren't thought of as a big deal for quite some time. Until that "personality" causes problems for one reason or another. Like Grampa wouldn't have approved of Cindy's new boyfriend, and now that muscle car mysteriously breaks down every time she tries to drive to his place. You get the idea.

Those are remnants. Those are no big deal. They can be pesky to chase down, when they have someplace big to run around in – or, say, when I couldn't encircle their chosen housing, like that furnace – but then it's just a matter of isolating them, severing their connections, and helping them move on.

Or stop existing. Whatever it is that happens when you die.

Revenants, though, those are another category altogether.

All right. Look. I'm not kidding when I say I don't know what comes next. All right? Just trying to be one hundred percent clear about this. And the reason I have to be one hundred percent *crystal* fucking clear about that is so you don't get the wrong impression about what I need to say next.

We don't like to admit this, but yes, it's possible to contact the dead. After a fashion.

See, yes, if we put in enough effort, we could summon up something like a shade of ... George Washington or Albert Einstein or Grampa or whoever. But what we'd really be doing is taking some kind of link – Grampa's muscle car or George Washington's wooden teeth, say – and summoning forth a kind of ... memory of them.

It would be ... a type of remnant. In other words, it would be incomplete. It would know some things, yes, but not others. Grampa might remember his car, or Washington how cold it was in Valley Forge, that kind of thing. A detail or two here and there. But that's about it.

Because it wouldn't *be* Grampa or George Washington. It would be a spirit constructed of memories from whatever links were available.

If the *true* spirit of Grampa or George Washington didn't just evaporate or something – if it moved on to reincarnate or visit some kind of afterlife but continues to exist – it's still out of our reach for *good*. Gone. Even the highest masters of necromancy admit that. Unless they're lying to their own adepts, and I don't see why they'd bother. Not like we can't keep a secret.

Now why is all that important? Why am I bothering to tell you about summoning up shades? Because you need to know it before I can explain revenants.

Revenants are a kind of self-created shade.

What that means is that someone – a wizard of some stripe, who only knows enough about necromancy to be dangerous – fears the great unknown of death and takes steps to try to prevent it ever happening to *them*.

Doesn't work, of course. Sooner or later, we all gotta die. Price of living in the first place.

But, if they're dedicated enough, and know enough magic, they can *sort of* accomplish their goal. Sort of.

What they end up doing is preparing a...

Okay, look. Yes, I know how it's done and no, I'm not going to tell you. You want to play that stupid game, you've gotta do your own damn homework for it.

Point is, after taking the necessary steps to prepare themselves, sooner or later, their body dies. And in that moment, those steps they took create a shade of themselves that they pretend goes on living. A shade that – depending on how good they were at their magic and how well-prepared they were before their demise took them – can be anywhere from about fifty percent to maybe ninety percent of who they were.

Usually, it's closer to fifty percent, but I've heard of some that pushed that ninety percent envelope pretty hard.

It's never a hundred percent, though. *Never*. Who you are changes and evolves with time, and revenants *do not*. They're little better than a fuzzy recording of who a person thinks they are at the time of death.

But they can be dangerous. Because usually they've got an agenda of some kind that they're not going to let a little thing like death stopping them from accomplishing.

And they retain at least *some* of their skill at magic.

In other words, my day was about to get a whole lot worse.

***

FIRST THING I HAD TO DO, THOUGH, WAS HAVE A SECOND MEETING WITH the two women. Because circumstances had *definitely* changed, and my original estimate – the one they approved – would no longer apply.

Hell, I deserved *combat pay* if I was going up against a revenant. Sadly, that wasn't an option. But neither was trying to pretend I was just clearing out a remnant or two, either.

So we gathered once more at that huge, teak table in the dining room that I was now certain was wider than architecture alone would support.

The older woman in her black dress and sweater – definitely suspicious colors, now that I had more confirmation that this household involved practitioners of some stripe – and the younger woman, Connie, supposedly, who had changed her clothes. Tan pants and a navy blue sweater now. But I could see a silver chain that disappeared inside the neck of that sweater, and I suspected that it ended in an amulet or talisman of some sort.

"There's a problem," I said.

Both of them sighed, but while the older woman only mumbled, "Of *course* there is," Connie said, louder, "What sort of problem?"

I explained about remnants and revenants and how I knew which had caused the loss of their furnace's fire elementals.

"So?" the older woman said, as though I hadn't just told her that she had some kind of sorcerous spirit loose in her home. "What difference does that really make?"

I checked myself from sighing in frustration. Wedged my professional smile into place.

"Because a remnant – even a *handful* of remnants – would be fairly simple to deal with, and within the boundaries of the work order we agreed to. A *revenant*, however, is much more *powerful* and much more *dangerous*. I couldn't possibly proceed without being properly compensated for my work."

"We have an agreement," the older woman said.

"You intend to insist on it?" I asked.

"I do," she confirmed with a decisive nod.

"All right," I said. "Let me tell you what that means. That means I'm going to go back into..." – *don't call it the creepy pet museum, don't call it the creepy pet museum* – "...the basement and check the area around your furnace for any remnants. Hell, I might even find one."

In that basement? I wouldn't be shocked if I found several.

"And when I do, I'll deal with it. And then I'll leave. And then you can bring back your elementalist, and pay them their rate to summon three brand-new c-grade salamanders for you, and bind them into that furnace. Might even work normally for a little while."

I shook my head. "But at some point – might be months, might be weeks, might be only *hours*, depending – your revenant may just decide it needs one or more of those fire elementals for its own purposes. When this happens – and given that it's taken three from you already, I see no reason to believe your revenant is finished with whatever it needs them for – your furnace will go down again. And the elementalist will tell you that the same problem recurred. And then you'll have to call in another—"

"You've made your point," Connie said.

"Have I?" I asked. "Because I don't know what connections you have that greenlit your getting three c-grade salamanders for this house" – I raised my hands defensively – "and I'm not asking. It's none of my business. But I can tell you that those connections will eventually start balking if you need too many of them."

Even the older woman frowned at that, as though she hadn't considered this angle on her problem. Which told me that their connections were pretty darned high up.

Still. I made a point of looking from Connie to the older woman and back.

"So," I said, in a more reasonable tone. "What's it going to be? New work order? Or stick to the one that will, at best, present a temporary fix without addressing your real problem?"

While they looked at one another – quite possibly holding a telepathic conversation to some degree, if they were adept enough – I shrugged and said, "Easier on me to stick with the current work order. I'll be done sooner. Might even get to squeeze in another job today. But, you know, professional ethics and all that."

"Hard to believe that a *necromancer* worries about ethics," the older woman said.

"And yet," I said with my best *fuck you* smile, "here we are."

"All right, all right," Connie said. "Mother, enough baiting our magitech. He's dealing squarely with us and you know it."

Now *that* was an interesting statement, and I *almost* called them on it. But I had a hunch that I'd be happier pretending I hadn't caught what I thought I'd just caught.

"We need our heat," Connie said, not with any special emphasis, but still I had the feeling that she was telling her mother something else, too. "And I see no point in throwing good money after a bad fix."

"But—"

"Let's at least discuss his estimate for our ... situation."

I laid it out for them. Wasn't pretty and it wasn't cheap. But given what I'd already had to say about revenants, Connie's mother had no right to that shocked look on her face.

The grim expression that Connie herself had was a lot more appropriate.

Though, honestly, it pissed me off a little bit anyway. I mean, these people had enough money to maintain space-warping spells for their *dining room*. They'd had *three* fire elementals handling the heat. And they'd paid for – and gotten permits for – *c-grade* salamanders for a private residence.

They had more than enough money to pay *my* fucking bill.

But then, I guess some people only stayed rich by stretching every penny further than ten freight trains could stretch that penny on a train track.

They were, at least, smart enough not to push back too hard. And in the end, they agreed to a reasonable fee, with reasonable potential cost overruns, depending on how much trouble the revenant gave me.

Then it was just a matter of going back out to the van, getting some extra reagents and paraphernalia I'd need, and then a quick call to the station to let them know what Dwayne had gotten me into out here, by accepting this gig on my behalf.

Then, it was time to start tracking down the revenant.

THE REVENANT HAD TO BE SOMEWHERE IN THE HOUSE.

Wait. Amend that slightly. The revenant was *most likely* somewhere in the house. Technically, it could probably leave the residence for short periods of time. Mostly at night, but on overcast days – and those rain clouds were overhead now, even though they had yet to start dumping down their rain on us – it could risk venturing out for short times as well. Long as it didn't get caught out in the sunlight.

Hard to emphasize enough to nonpractitioners just how important natural sunlight is to restricting the movement of the undead. Got nothing to do with ultraviolet rays or whatever other nonsense people theorized for a while there, a few years back.

Truth is, the sun was the first god known to protohumans. Before the idea of worship or gods were fully formed in the minds of our evolutionary forebears, the rising sun and its presence in the sky were sources of joy and safety. Not to mention new beginnings, life, and more.

Those associations run deeper in us than thought or emotion.

And they contain a great deal of power for restricting the dead. Not necessarily *destroying* them – though that *can* happen sometimes – but primarily *hindering* them. *Weakening* them.

The undead – which includes even remnants, but extends to revenants and other types as well – require some kind of physical anchor to maintain their integrity. Professionally, we call those things *tokens*. I've already told you something about them. To that you can now add that tokens hold the undead together, against the natural pull to, well, move on is as good a phrase as any.

Tokens can act as a form of housing for them. A place to hide, and recuperate the energies they expend just to continue on. To say nothing of the kind of activity that gets called "haunting" or, say, using magic to break the bonds of elemental spirits and give them new tasks.

So there was a chance that the revenant would venture out today, while the sun was hidden behind storm clouds, far more likely that it was in the house. Possibly in its token.

And in this house overflowing with knickknacks and bric-a-brac – a house clearly occupied by practitioners of some stripe – there might be a *number* of tokens. Not to mention fetishes and amulets, which could be mistaken for tokens on initial sighting. Meaning there might be rooms full of red herrings I needed to find some way to avoid.

Because sooner or later, that revenant was going to realize I was coming for it. And it would begin to work against me.

I needed to start by finding some way to get a sense of it.

Which meant I had to go back into that godawful pet museum with its dried blood-looking paint job. Because the last place I'd known for certain that the revenant had been was at that furnace. Likely my best chance of gaining some sense of the revenant would be down there.

And if I was lucky, I could learn what I needed to without having to encircle the furnace or mess with the work of the elementalists.

But I definitely needed to look it over.

Which meant it was time to open myself to the deeper perceptions.

Personally, I always do that starting with hearing. I find I can pick up some things faster by hearing them than I can with other senses. Natural inclination, I suppose.

So I turned to face the furnace. Set my bag on the dark red limestone beside me. Sat cross-legged on the floor.

I focused myself through a couple of deep breaths. Let myself first become aware of the physical sounds about me. My heartbeat. My breathing. The faint creak of the house above. The slight hiss of pipes moving water.

Moving my attention into the etheric and nearby astral, I first listened for the psychic armor I wore whenever I was out on a professional gig. The kind of thing that would protect me from surprises, whether through happenstance or ill-intent.

My armor always sounded to me like the ring of a blacksmith's hammer on properly heated, high-quality steel. Not the sound of the contact itself but the ring that echoes *just* before the sound dies away in anticipation of the next strike.

I acclimated myself to that ring. Then eliminated it from my considerations.

The next sounds to draw my attention were the ones I didn't want to hear. The snuffling of curious Labradors. The inquisitive sounds of cats.

At least a dozen of those ... museum displays still had remnants of their animals attached to them.

I'll admit it. I wanted to stop what I was doing and help whatever little bits of those domestic animals – what I devoutly hoped had been happy and well-loved pets – move on. But irritated as I'd been in redoing the work order, I'd excluded remnants from it. So I couldn't do it. And I had to listen past them.

The faint hint of chanting in Latin. Male voice. On the deep side.

Helpful, yes, but I couldn't pick out enough character in the voice to use it as a marker. To track from it.

So I had to cycle through my other senses.

Smell and taste both gave me hints of sulfur, which isn't nearly as bad as it might sound. Sulfur is often used in working with fire

elementals, especially those of a Western European bent, like salamanders. I could learn something about the working in there, but not
enough about the revenant itself.

Really, all the smells told me was that it was powerful enough to
pull together and work with essential sulfur – its astral essence, if you
will – which wasn't much of a surprise. I mean, considering it
managed to snag three c-grade salamanders, I already knew this
revenant had something going for it.

From touch, I picked up a hint of clamminess inside heat. Which
suggested that the revenant had been pushing itself in this working.

That was good. That was very good. That told me that the
revenant would need serious recovery time. Which meant ...
assuming Connie and her mother had gotten the elementalist out for
next day service ... it had been two to three days since those salamanders went missing. And proper recovery for a revenant who pushes as
hard as I now believed this one had would require a full quarter-
moon cycle.

All right, look. I could give you the whole formal lecture about
moon cycles, magic and the dead, but it gets pretty technical. So,
really, you're better off just trusting me on this one. Suffice to say
that, without a body of its own – and a token didn't count for this, I
mean without a *living body of its own* – the revenant and its magic
would be even more tied to lunar cycles than a good deal of human
magic was.

I moved on to sight which, unfortunately, was both helpful and
unhelpful for me.

Sight told me that the revenant had been an older man when he
died, with a long full head of hair and beard to match, and the kind
of big body I associated with those who described themselves as
having "a zest for life."

That part was helpful.

But the image wasn't clear enough for me to pick out any special
tool or jewelry that might indicate a likely token for me to find.

Which meant that, unless this revenant was tied to a freaking
picture, sight hadn't given me anything actionable.

In fact, I hadn't really learned anything *actionable* from studying the furnace.

Which meant that unless I came up with something brilliant, I'd be stuck going room to room and checking everything that could possibly be this thing's token.

The professional equivalent of a death by a thousand cuts.

I had to think of something good. Fast.

* * *

EVERY ONCE IN A WHILE, EVEN A SCHLUB LIKE ME CAN HAVE A MOMENT of brilliance.

And I had one right then.

When the revenant had done its ritual to steal the elementals, it had left enough of a signature to *detect*, but not to *track*.

Not enough for *me* to track, at least.

But here in this room, with the right senses opened, I could hear the snuffling of three different Labrador retriever remnants.

Hunting dogs. That existed only as remnants, yes, but what remained of them worked on the same plane of existence as that revenant.

And the hunting instinct is a core element of the Labrador retriever. *Any* Lab remnant will still possess it.

In some ways, I'd even be doing those poor Lab remnants a favor, bringing them into this hunt. I'd be giving them something to do, other than hang out here, where the smells – outside of my own – had to be old and boring to them by now.

Had to do this carefully, though...

All right. First things had to come first. And that meant gathering those three snuffling remnant hounds.

Much as I'd like to tell you this was difficult, maybe even danger-ous, I'd be lying through my teeth. Remnants are very easy to work with. Which is one of the reasons that some practitioners – and I'd be very much surprised if Connie and her mother didn't know about the ones down here – keep them around.

So really, it was just a question of pulling a small leather thong from my work bag, carving a few symbols into it with the point of my black-handled dagger while filling the thong with the right twist of power – stuff any novice necromancer could do (though no novice could do it as quickly or efficiently as I could, thank you very much).

Then, after slinging my bag back over my shoulder, I just had to tune my senses to each snuffler in turn, and reach out to them with an invitation, through the prepared thong. Which they now saw as a leash, and me as taking them on at least a walk.

Easy as handing out free money on a streetcorner.

With my senses opened – limitedly, because I didn't want to see the rest of the room's remnants, they'd just make me sad – I could now perceive the three Labs as half-faded images of the dogs they'd been in life. Grizzled old gents in retriever terms. A little on the hefty side, with graying muzzles, and a tendency towards farts that didn't smell any better now that they were dead.

I gave them a moment while they snuffled at each other in the ways that all dogs acquainted themselves with new friends, for now they could perceive each other easily enough. All tethered to my thong as they were.

Then, I pulled together my impressions of the sorcerous revenant spirit. Everything I'd been able to pick up about it through each sense, whether I personally found that information useful or not.

I breathed those impressions into my hand, the closest I could come to holding an article of the revenant's clothing. I offered my impressions to the three Labs.

Their instincts kicked in immediately, and three not-actually-moist-but-feeling-moist-in-the-moment snouts snuffled my hand, gathering what I could give them.

Before I could even consider issuing any instructions, all three then pushed past me to the furnace, and began snuffling it intently. Presumably filling in blanks that my limited senses missed but their own could detect.

Disturbingly, they then yipped happily. As though this revenant were a known and loved master.

My stomach sank at that thought. I'd been hoping they wouldn't know him. Silly hope maybe, but when out in the field, I tend to find hope wherever I can.

If the dogs didn't know the revenant, they might not care one way or the other what happened when I caught up with it.

But if they'd loved that revenant in life, then the price I'd pay for tracking it down quickly would be to bring it three potential allies.

And this was getting worse and worse.

<hr>

SPEAKING OF THINGS GETTING WORSE.

Those remnant Labs? They led me out of the furnace, up the stairs and into the house proper.

Where Connie's mother was.

She clucked her tongue at me – as though I were some inter-loping servant and not the magitech they'd *hired* to solve a *problem* for them – and started dithering in my wake as though she expected me to start trashing the place if not watched *constantly*.

And with my deeper senses open somewhat, I could see now that she was, in fact, a Witch. As in, an adherent of the Old Religion – or old-ish, in the strictest technical sense, unless her family was one of those rare few that honestly never did stop practicing, Inquisitions and Age of Enlightenment and so forth be damned – and practitioner of a ... flexible sort of earth magic that could cover nuances well outside its normal field.

Those old systems of study were pretty haphazard, compared with modern techniques. But they did occasionally provide surprises. And I was in no mood for surprises.

I tried not to worry about that, though, and just focused on following my hounds, as they led me through an elegant living room that smelled of recent dragon's blood incense...

...and straight to a wood-paneled wall. A wall that should've been the back wall of the house.

I looked down at the spectral hounds leashed to my small leather thong.

They stared back, wondering what the hold-up was.

I sighed and started looking for the catch, lever, button, or whatever it was that would open this particular concealed door.

"Just what exactly do you think you're doing?" Connie's mother asked, from behind me.

"I *think* I'm trying to open what obviously must be a concealed door. Though you're welcome to help with this, if you think you can stand it."

"Perhaps you have only read the word in context," she said, "and developed a misunderstanding of its meaning. The word 'obvious' means—"

"I'm acquainted with its proper meaning, thank you very much."

"Clearly you are not, or you would know that if that wall were obviously a door, you would not need to hunt a means of opening it."

I sighed and looked back at her. "So you're not going to help me with this door then?"

Connie's mother merely looked back at me, as though I were a truculent child she had no intention of indulging.

I didn't buy it. I felt certain she knew this door was there. And the Labs were getting restless. So I turned back to my check—

—and found it. A place where two bits of wood paneling came together in such a way as to conceal a small pressure plate.

I looked back at Connie's mother and pressed the plate.

A common-door-sized portion of the wall opened inward, leading to a poorly lit set of stairs that led up and to the left. Stairs that, properly speaking, should've been outside the house, but were not.

Yeah, these people were playing a lot of games with space. Expensive games. If I ever came back here, I fully intended to up my rates for them.

The dogs and I started forward.

"Stop right there," Connie's mother said in an impressively commanding voice.

I almost pushed on anyway. My work order gave me permission to track down the revenant. Nothing was said about limitations or places I could not follow it, if needed.

But even for us necromancers, customer service was customer service.

So I frustrated my hunting pack by turning back to face Connie's mother.

"What?" I asked impatiently.

Yeah, in case you hadn't guessed, customer service was never my strongest suit.

"Where, exactly, do you think you're going?"

"Madam, I am going wherever I need to, to track down that revenant and deal with it."

"You have no need to go up those stairs. Do your job from here."

"That's not how this works," I said. But before I could continue, she cut in.

"You are a necromancer, are you not?"

"Are you going to get mad again if I say 'obviously?'"

"You summon the dead, yes?"

"I can summon shades of the dead, yes, but that's not germane to this situation."

She clucked her tongue. "A revenant is dead. You summon the dead. Therefore, you can summon this revenant and deal with it right here, if necessary. You have no reason to go rummaging through my house."

"I'm hardly rummaging," I said. "The only thing I care about is finding the token associated with that revenant. You know, the thing I'd need to summon it here, to me?"

She scoffed. "I hardly think—"

"Unless, of course, you have some other link you can provide me to this revenant? Because all I have to go on are some vague impressions that I was able to gather downstairs. Which would not have been even close to enough, were I not a *clever* enough necromancer to figure out how I could use them to suit my needs."

"If you expect to impress me by heaping praise upon yourself for a job unfinished, you're quite mistaken."

"If you think impressing you is important to me, *you're* the one who is quite mistaken. I'm just here to do a job. And you're interfering with it."

"I won't have you going up those stairs."

"Then I'll have to invoke clause seventeen-b in our work order agreement."

"Which is?"

"What happens when the client – that's you – refuses to allow me access I require to complete my task. I'll leave, and you'll be billed for my time, along with the kill fee listed in that section, for my trouble."

"We won't pay it."

I gave her an evil smile. "We can take this to an adjudicator, if you like. I guarantee you you'll lose, no matter how much leeway you think money gives you. I will document where you stopped me, and why, and detail exactly how your obstinacy interfered with the work. Truth does have a certain ring to it, you know, that those trained in adjudication can hear."

She frowned, and flared her nostrils at me. But before she could get out whatever she had to say next, I had one more bomb to drop on her.

"Oh, and given the nature of the counter-complaint *I'd* be lodging, *none* of the magitech guilds are likely to work with you until the matter is resolved. And when I win, which I will, you'll find that only the lesser guilds will be willing to work for you in the future. At least, until you've finished paying me not only for my time and the kill fee, but whatever additional penalties the adjudicator orders."

I admit it. My smile stretched into a grin then. "Among the elementalists, those lesser guilds won't be able to get you anything better than g-grade salamanders. If that."

G-grade were the sort used for one-room studio apartments. And those apartments were rarely all that comfortable.

Connie's mother narrowed her eyes at me now.

"You're the one who wants to play hardball," I said with a shrug. "I'm just as happy getting my job done and getting out of here."

"And what guarantee do I have that you'll respect our privacy?"

"Well, I could just point out that I don't give a lesser damn about your personal peccadilloes. Because I don't. But if that's not enough, there's the reputation of Curwin Necromantic to consider. If our magitechs went around blabbing about the odd stuff we saw on the job, nobody'd hire us."

Well. I mean, *obviously* – which is a word I know quite well how to use, thank you – we magitechs discuss these things among ourselves. But we don't name names and we don't write memoirs.

She gave a hesitant nod. "Then I suppose—"

"Oh, before you finish that thought," I said. "I presume it goes without saying that if I see anything *illegal*, I'll have no choice but to report it to the proper authorities."

She actually considered that, which disturbed me. "Anything recognizably illegal, you mean."

My turn to scoff. "Look. You want examples? Well I know what growing mandrake looks like—"

"Mandrake is a *controlled* substance, not an *illegal* substance."

"—and if I see you growing any, I'll ask to see your permits. But that's only one example. I mean, I also recognize black cat bone—"

"Black *cat* bone?" she said, looking properly disgusted at least.

"Specifically violates the Black Magic Act."

"What would make you think that was even a *possibility* here?"

"Two of the taxidermied cats in the basement are black. I had to consider it a possibility."

"You are a disgusting man to think we would even *consider* so abusing our beloved animals."

"Glad to hear it," I said. "But now that we understand each other, can I go do my job?"

"You might as well wait a moment first," she said, sounding tired. "I'll get the copies of our permits to grow mandrake, datura, and a few other things. Better to save the time now."

THEY HAD PERMITS TO GROW TWENTY-SEVEN DIFFERENT CONTROLLED herbs and plants. Twenty-seven. Somewhere while reviewing those permits, I wondered just who these people were. And I don't just mean the names on the forms, either. But by the time I reached the last permit, I decided I was better off knowing as little about these people as I could get away with.

One way or the other, those permits were all valid and up-to-date. So once we'd finished going through those, I was finally allowed to take my long-suffering remnant hunting hounds up those stairs.

Though Connie's mother *did* make me take off my shoes – and cautioned me once more about my promised privacy – before letting me proceed in my stocking feet.

Remember how I said there seemed to be too many gables on this house? There's a reason for that. There turned out to be a whole nother floor not visible from the street. All of it – walls, floor and ceiling – paneled in what looked to be Douglas fir. Probably from trees that had grown on the property. Possibly trees that had been cleared to make room for this house...

Smelled of fir and walnut oil. Half-expected the hall at the top of the stairs to be lit by candles, but no. Soft, yellow light bulbs that only *looked* like candles in sconces.

Religious artwork on the walls, depicting the family's various gods, rites performed in the woods by moonlight, that kind of thing.

Six doorways led off of the hall, three on each side, and none of them with doors. Only at the end of the hall – a good sixty feet away, I didn't even want to *think* about what all this space-warping cost – did I see even a single door.

I did hear some soft chanting, and the gentle padding of bare feet on a wooden floor, coming from the first doorway to my left.

The remnant hounds were all about going farther down the hall, but I couldn't resist glancing through that one doorway.

Found out then what Connie's mother had been so concerned about me seeing. Connie herself was performing some kind of religious ritual. And doing it "skyclad," as the Witches say.

Doubt Connie's mother would believe me, but I was more interested in making a quick note of how much and what kind of power she was raising, than in worrying about how Connie looked naked. I had a girlfriend of my own, and didn't need to go looking at other women.

Connie was doing a sort of slow-burn power raising in a cone shape, bordered by the confines of the circle she danced in.

I'd seen this type of thing before. The quality of the power raised was far more important than its quantity, and entirely religious. She wasn't casting spells and she wasn't doing anything that would interfere with my work. She was engaged in an act of religious devotion, contained entirely within her circle. Nothing more.

I moved on then, and my remnant hunting Labs were focused on the last doorway on the left.

I had a bad feeling about what I'd find in that room. This whole floor was ... concerning. Why did they need a hidden floor for their temple room? Witchcraft was a common religion these days. Yeah, I got why they'd hide their controlled plants. That might've been a deal worked out with the county or state as a requirement for the sheer number of permits they needed.

But so far, that only covered two, maybe three of these doorways.

Three. The greenhouse was on the right-hand side, and it *was* a greenhouse. Lots of glass, letting me both see and hear the rain now pouring down.

Curious as part of me was, though, I didn't look in the other doorways as I passed. The rest of me just had too strong a feeling that I was better off not knowing what I'd find.

...well, maybe I'd have a peek on the way back.

We reached the last doorway, though, and the remnant Labs made clear that *this* was the doorway we wanted. Not the door at the end, which would have been my guess. Just because a single closed door on a floor like this seemed ominous to me.

Still, no way I was bringing these Labs into that room with me.

Honestly, what I wanted to do was help them move on. But that was a murky area, contractually, and given the way Connie's mother had been acting, I didn't want to give her anything like justifiable cause for complaint.

So instead I set the binding thong along the wall between this doorway and the one before it.

"Sit," I said to the remnant hounds. "Stay."

They couldn't travel far from the thong anyway, but I hoped that reinforcing that fact with commands they *had* to have been trained with in life would help keep them out of the way.

Then, girding myself against what I might find, I entered that last room on the left.

This room was painted matte black. Floors, walls, ceiling. All of it. No electric lights in here. No windows, either. Only black pillar candles, wall-mounted holders made from brass, one in the center of each wall. Currently unlit.

I could see cabinets along the outside wall – or what was *likely* an outside wall, tough to be certain in this house. Likely holding ritual implements and the like. Also likely where I'd find the revenant's token.

A circle and a triangle had been painted on the floor in silver paint, which suggested even to mundane eyes – *knowledgeable* mundane eyes, at least – that this room was for summonings.

I could detect the faint whiff of old livestock. That smell I associated with county fairs as a child, which was the only place a city boy like me saw real goats and cows and such. And underneath that, the smell of old blood as well.

Well, at least it wasn't likely that they were sacrificing dogs and cats. Not the way these remnant Labs wanted to get to their old master, whom they were *certain* was in that room.

And technically, sacrificing chickens, goats and the like was legal. Sort of.

It was legal when done for *religious* purposes, the way it was in Vodou, Candomblé, Umbanda, Lukumi and the other African Diasporic religions.

The kind of Witchcraft Connie was doing in that other room, though, did not generally include animal sacrifices.

But – and this was the loophole that doubtless Connie's mother was sailing a freaking *battleship* through right now – I didn't *know* the strictures of their religion. Which meant I didn't *know* that those strictures didn't include animal sacrifice.

Which meant I didn't *know* they were doing anything illegal. And had no reason to run to the cops.

Of course, I now had every expectation that Connie's mother's delays had been all about establishing what I was likely to go to the cops over and what I wasn't, before she'd risk my running across a room where they likely summoned demons.

Mind you, despite the common misbelief, even demon summoning did not necessarily violate the Black Magic Act. It came down to what they wanted the demon for. What task they'd set it.

But here's the thing. If you wanted one of the demons from, say, Solomon's famous books to help you learn French or find you lost treasure or something like that, you wouldn't need to offer them a life.

Blood sacrifices *combined* with demon summoning was a pretty strong indicator of violating the Black Magic Act. Because they only demanded blood to do some pretty nasty stuff.

But again, nothing here constituted *proof* of a crime. Only a strong suggestion.

All the same, I gave that room a once-over with my deeper senses before entering.

First thing I heard were echoes of frightened goats and chickens, in their last moments. Not remnants, you understand. What I was hearing was nothing that remained of those poor animals. It's just that in my line of work, we develop increased sensitivity to anything relating to the deceased.

Beyond that, I could hear echoes of commanding Latin in a deep voice, giving orders to things that had been called forth into that triangle.

Past the physical, I could smell dry scents. Reptilian. And musky scents, leonine. Others as well. Likely those things that had been called into that triangle. The reptilian scents especially clung to my tongue.

Reaching out with my sense of touch, then, I immediately realized I could feel a presence in that room.

And then I understood.

The revenant's token. It wasn't *in* this room. The token *was* this room.

I COULD SEE THE REVENANT NOW. LIKE A FADED, SEMI-TRANSPARENT photograph of the man he'd been in life. Tall. Maybe half-a-head taller than me, and hefty as he was, that made him seem huge. His face had been ruddy and lined around the eyes. His hair had been grayed out from what might have once been jet black, leaving it like a coat of shaggy fur that only grew out of his scalp, cheeks and chin.

Well, and above his eyes. Because those eyebrows were like hairy caterpillars.

The revenant appeared to be wearing a blood red robe, with planetary and elemental symbols embroidered in gold thread. The hood fell behind him like a mini-cape.

Interesting that whatever remained of this man felt most natural and comfortable in a ritual robe, holding a black-handled kris dagger whose black blade looked to be stained. I supposed that tracked with the fact that his freaking token was his ritual room.

I'd never even *heard* of something like this before. A room as a token for a revenant. I'd have to write an article for our monthly journal, *A Bone to Pick*. (Yes, that would be allowed by the work order, because all identifying information would be stripped from the article.)

First, though, I had to deal with this revenant.

And now that I could sense him, I could feel that he had considerable power, for a dead man.

"You are most unkind, necromancer," the revenant said. "To bring my dogs so close to me, yet still keep us apart."

Before I could give him a witty rejoinder, he whipped his ritual dagger through a cutting motion while mouthing words I could have said for him, had I a mind to.

He was fast on the draw, for a revenant. And he severed my thong's tie to the remnant hounds.

Then a cluck of his tongue was all he needed for what little remained of those three grizzled old retrievers to zip past me into the room, tails and tongues wagging as they jumped up on their master.

To his credit, the revenant actually seemed happy to see them. He crouched down and set down his dagger to scratch and pet his dogs with both hands.

My turn for the unexpected quick move. A gesture and a pulse of power was enough to pull the ephemeral remains of that dagger to me, and a chanting pass of my obsidian wand – slid down into my right hand from its hiding place up my sleeve – dissolved the dagger into nothingness.

That drew the revenant's attention back to me. Still crouching, he stopped petting his dogs and gave me a dark look.

"A tool is just a tool, necromancer," he said, standing.

"For *me*, a tool is just a tool," I said. "But that dagger was a part of you that you chose to separate from. Only for a moment, yes, but enough of a disconnection from your will that I—"

"I am no neophyte," the revenant said. "I understand what just happened here. I am reminding *you* that as parts of me go, it was a least part. And worth paying for the confirmation of your purpose here. You mean to end me, and I will not end so quietly."

"That doesn't *have* to be how this goes down," I said, shaking my head just enough to add emphasis.

"Spare me your lies," the revenant said.

"No lies," I said simply. "I'm here to solve a problem. A problem that began with you. Now, it's true that the quick and easy answer to most necromantic problems is to track down whatever spiritual leftovers are causing problems and help them move on. Which is what I fully expected to do here."

He cocked a thick, shaggy eyebrow at me. "Your application of the past tense has been noted."

"I didn't want to bring you the dogs, because I didn't want to give you allies. In case this came to a fight. But it's clear that, in life, you loved those dogs. And they loved you. And anybody that animals love can't be *all* bad. Which means that maybe I can consider other options here."

"If you're willing to consider other options, why deprive me of my dagger?"

"Multiple reasons. But the most important at the moment was to make sure you knew I could do it. I've found over the years that some adepts ... are hesitant to believe in the skills of others."

"They are fools then, to let arrogance blind them so. The underestimated foe is the most dangerous."

I could have said the same for the overestimated foe, but didn't want to get into a debate with the incomplete memory of a dead man.

"What are the others of these 'multiple reasons?'"

"We'll get to them. We have other things we need to discuss first."

"Such as?"

"Why are you here? You obviously devoted a good deal of time and effort to making sure a portion of you—"

"*All* of me, thank you," he interrupted stiffly.

"—survived death. Which suggests that you have unfinished business to take care of. I'd like to know what that business is."

"My affairs are my own."

"They *were* your own," I said flatly. "But then you stole three c-grade salamanders from what I presume are your inheritors."

"I commissioned those salamanders. That I passed beyond the veil—"

"*This* part of you hasn't passed beyond *any* veil. You're still here."

"*That I passed beyond the veil* does not make this house or its contents any less my own."

"Legally, that's a dubious statement," I said. "But let's speak practically, for the moment. Do you need this house kept warm?"

"I am beyond such petty needs."

"Connie – assuming that's really her name – and her mother are not. They need that furnace in good working order. And now it has no salamanders. Because you ... repurposed them."

His face wrinkled at the business jargon turn of phrase, and I couldn't blame him. But he'd done what he'd done.

"Then let them bring in more."

I shook my head. "You broke the bindings used by the contractors you'd hired. They won't reinstate those bindings, much less summon up three more *c-grade* fire elementals until they are assured the same thing won't happen again."

"Once the salamanders are mine, it's no one's business what I do with them."

"That's ... not true of *any* spirits. We have laws in this country—"

"I didn't break any."

"Maybe, maybe not," I said. "But if you commissioned that furnace, then you know the restrictions put on c-grade elementals. Now, I don't know what you *did* with them—"

"Nor shall you."

"—so I don't *know* that the use they were put to is illegal."

"It was not."

"*My point is*," I said sharply. "The elementalists won't give you any *more* elementals until *I* certify that the problem has been solved. And it won't happen again."

"Ah. And I'm 'the problem,' am I?"

"You've already admitted you took the salamanders. So, yes."

"So," the revenant said, idly patting one dog with one hand and stroking his beard with the other. "What do you see as the options for resolving the 'problem' you say I present."

"First, I'm not the one saying it. Connie and her mother are saying it. I'm the second magitech they brought in to deal with it. Though, obviously, the first was an elementalist."

"Very well. Point granted."

Sucker actually sounded grudging and condescending at the same time. Made me *really* tempted to narrow those options down quickly.

But that would've been unprofessional.

"First option, of course, would be to help you move on. To help you leave this world behind, and ascend to the next great adventure."

Yes. I was, in fact, lying through my teeth about the "next great adventure." I wasn't dealing with a person, after all. I was dealing with a person's spiritual echo. I didn't owe him squat.

"I have no interest in moving to the next plane of existence at this time. I still have work to do here."

"And now we get to the first sticking point," I said with a sigh. "Because if you want to stay, I need to know what work that is."

"No, you don't."

"Yes. I do. Because if it turns out to be illegal and I didn't stop you, that's on me."

"I can guarantee you that my business is not illegal."

"Yeah, you're already in a gray area legally, after taking those elementals. So I'm afraid your word is not sufficient here."

"What more can you have of me than my word?"

"If I'm going to consider not helping you move on, legally I am required to read you."

"To read me what?"

I shook my head. "Not read something *to* you. I am required to read *you*."

THIS IS PART OF WHAT I HATE ABOUT DEALING WITH REVENANTS. There's enough of the person left over that I can almost forget I'm talking to a spiritual echo. Until I bump up against one of the ... incomplete sections, if you will.

See, in life, this revenant – for all his airs – was no expert in necromancy. (Demonology, maybe, but that's a different kettle of heavily armed squid.) Which means that what little he'd known in life got no priority except as necessary to help him "achieve" his current state.

Which meant that making the explanation *not* sound like gibberish to his revenant wasn't easy.

Sad, really, because the concept itself is pretty simple.

See, one thing I *can* tell you about what's necessary to force a revenant of yourself to exist after death is that it requires a *purpose*. Some great, powerful, driving *need* that pushes you to try to cram some bit of yourself into existence even when the real you dies.

Revenge is a common one. If anything about revenants could be considered *common*. See, practitioners of magic may come from all walks of life, but one thing many have in common is a … tendency toward arrogance. Even hotheadedness.

And so there's a … not inconsiderable segment among the practitioners of the world that push the legal limits constraining the ways they can wage magical war on each other.

Seriously. It's a major problem.

If this particular revenant existed to get revenge, I'd have no choice but to *make* him move on. End. Whatever. Guild rules wouldn't let me do anything else here.

I didn't mention that part, of course. Because there are so many ways that some practitioners attack each other with magic that *aren't* illegal – they *should* be, but good luck getting the votes for it – they forget that all the loopholes that let them do it while alive seal shut once they die.

The dead aren't supposed to go hassling the living. Nobody disputes that, even if those who create their own revenants might *forget* that little detail.

Anyway. When a practitioner *makes* a revenant through magic, that driving purpose gets embedded in it like an ectoplasmic blood type. And I was just the spiritual phlebotomist the situation called for.

"So it will be like allowing you to read my mind," the revenant said again. Likely because this was the closest it could come to understanding.

"Something like that," I said. "But not your thoughts. More like … your emotional drive. The way some are driven for knowledge, or others for fame and so on."

"And I must allow you to encircle me for this?"

"Sadly, it's a requirement."

"How can I trust that you will do nothing more than what we discuss?"

I gave a frustrated scoff. "You and your family. I freaking swear. If trust were red phosphorous, the whole lot of you combined wouldn't have enough to light a match."

"We have reasons for our caution."

"Then reason your way through this. I am *trying* to find a way to resolve this situation without *requiring* you to move on. But if it's going to work, you're going to *have* to work with me. And that means extending me some trust. If you're not willing to do that, let's just drop the pretense and—"

"Oh, very well." The revenant shook its head. "You're really quite a dramatic individual."

And the ironic statement award goes to...

I shook that line of thought away. "The circle, if you'd please."

The revenant, and the three remnant Labs all moved into that silver circle.

Now, alas, I finally had to enter that black room.

Felt a chill the moment I did, that had everything to do with the purposes this room had been put to. The things that had been summoned here.

Never was all that comfortable with spirits that were never alive. Part of the reason I didn't branch out into more elemental work, even though I could get higher rates if I were certified journeyman level or better at both.

I could've used the candles they had along the walls, but honestly I wanted to touch as little in here as I could get away with. I didn't even like using their *circle*, but if I didn't I'd probably offend the revenant. And I didn't need it to be in any more of a confrontational mood than was absolutely necessary.

I pulled out six white tea lights from my work bag. The revenant sniffed at the sight of them, but he didn't need to lug around a bag full of equipment from job to job. Tea lights were small, light, and did the job for most things.

I arrayed them around the circle, adding to each a pinch of sulfur. Then I added a line of sulfur to the silver circle itself, functionally drawing my own circle on top of it.

Strictly speaking, I didn't need to use sulfur for this. Salt would've been better. But the revenant would've taken salt as aggression – it's famous for its uses against the dead – and sulfur would've felt more familiar to it.

Then I lit the candles, going clockwise around the circle, adding a touch of power to each candle before lighting it, and pulling that power along the circle as I went.

"Not the most efficient approach," the revenant critiqued as I worked. I stuck to the low chant that would help establish this as my circle and under my control.

Just in case the revenant got any ... untoward notions.

Once the circle was complete, I thrust one hand at the revenant and spoke in Greek, the professional language of American necromancy.

"Spirit within spirit.
Mind within mind.
Purpose beneath all.
You permeate this ephemeral shell.
Come forth now, purpose.
Come forth now, drive.
Come forth now, need within all
And be writ large and plain before me."

The sulfur of the circle itself flared bright, trailing smoke that flowed together and wrote words in the air between the revenant and myself.

I must accomplish the Great Work, or all has been for nothing.

A sudden wave of sadness passed through me. I'd like to think I could keep it from my face, but the revenant immediately picked up that something was wrong.

Clearly this guy had practiced Western ritual magic when he was alive. Possibly in the tradition of those Golden Dawn types, or maybe the Argentum Astrum, or one of the other famous occult lodges of the twentieth century.

And among those types, that phrase – the Great Work – meant something very specific.

I really wanted to be wrong about this.

"The Great Work?" I asked. "By that do you mean achieving knowledge and conversation of your Holy Guardian Angel?"

"What else *could* I possibly mean?"

"Um," I said, and swallowed. "Hate to say this, but you're dead. You're—"

"I have *survived* death! I have *defeated* death. And now I shall accomplish *this* as well."

"You're *not a complete person* anymore. You're a fragment of your-self. What you're trying to do takes a lot of work for the *living*. For you, for what you are now, I'm pretty sure this is impossible."

"Spare me the limited perspective of your incomplete mastery of the Ars Magica."

I sighed. "What the hell did that have to do with…" I shook my head as understanding washed over me. "The salamanders were a distraction, weren't they? They were too powerful and too near. You couldn't eliminate them from your meditations."

The revenant frowned and stroked his beard. "It was … proving more difficult than I anticipated, yes. So they had to be dismissed."

"You *do* realize that Connie and her mother want to bring in more to replace them."

"Well, then they'll have to settle for d-grade. Or perhaps e-grade… No. I should be able to account for the presence of d-grade elementals."

"'Should' isn't good enough. If I certify that d-grade will work and you dismiss them, they'll call me back out and I'll have no choice left but to help you move on."

"If you can."

My turn for a glower. And I'd had more than a little practice glow-ering at the recalcitrant dead.

"Let us understand something, you and I. Whatever you were in life – whatever magics you commanded – no longer matters, where I am concerned. I am a necromancer. I am a lord of death. You are just another spirit to me. Test that at your peril."

He tried to stare me down then, but my anger was up. And whatever sense of self-preservation existed in that revenant came to the fore.

"Very well. What do you require of me?"

"You stand within the circle of my power. If you will swear two oaths, my magic will enforce them and I can consider this matter concluded. You'll be able to get on with your attempt at the Great Work."

"What is the first oath?"

"That from this moment forward and lasting for so long as you remain on this plane of existence, you will not interfere magically with any of this house's elemental spirits."

"But if—"

"If they bring in elementals that interfere with your meditations, you must seek resolution by *asking* those identified to me as Connie and her mother to have those elementals dismissed and replaced by certified *living* professionals."

"Must I swear to that part?"

I sighed and shook my head. "So long as you swear not to magically interfere, I don't care about the rest."

"Very well, I swear that from that from this moment forward, for so long as I remain on this plane of existence, I shall take no action to magically interfere with any elementals or other spirits bound within this house. Good enough?"

"Better than I expected. Thank you."

The revenant nodded its head graciously. "What is next?"

"Do you swear that you seek only to complete the Great Work? And that once you complete it you shall move on to what comes next?"

"I shall do so happily. Yes. I swear that I remain on this plane of existence for the sole purpose of completing the Great Work, and that I shall move on to what comes next once I complete it."

Two oaths, both now magically sealed by my own power. Which left only one other matter.

"All right," I said. "Those are enough to deal with the reasons I was brought here. But unfortunately, the law requires me to see about one more thing before I go."

"What thing is that?" the revenant asked suspiciously.

"Are you willing to let me bind you against harming others who do not bring harm to you first, beginning this day and continuing for so long as you remain on this plane of existence?"

The revenant huffed. "Honestly? This is a legal requirement?"

"It most definitely is. If I leave a revenant to its business and then it hurts someone, I can be held accountable."

"And once this is done, I shall be rid of you?"

"That's right. Once we've taken care of this, I can leave you alone."

"Then I shall agree to it. Get on with your binding and let me get on with my work."

Truth was, I felt a little guilty about letting the revenant remain, trying to accomplish an impossible task until it lost cohesion on its own. But I'd solved the problem. Which was all they'd asked of me.

At least, so long as Connie and her mother agreed.

AFTER I PUT THOSE REMNANT HOUNDS BACK IN THE BASEMENT, I ONCE more found myself back at that too-big teak table, in a dining room that couldn't exist without magic.

Honestly, the way this house had to thrum with magic at all these space-warping spells, it was no wonder that guy'd died without completing the Great Work. He'd've done better to set himself up with a tiny house or a shed or something, even here on the property, and working there.

Anyway, Connie's mother was still in all black, at the other end of the table from me. Connie was dressed again, but in a simple white linen robe.

"All right," I said. "I've tracked the problem to its source. Do you need me to tell you whose spirit resides in your upstairs ritual room?"

"We do not," Connie's mother said, and Connie merely nodded agreement.

"Well, that spirit is trying to complete the Great Work, which the living man had not completed before dying."

"Can he do it?" Connie asked quietly.

"No," I said. "I'm sorry, but only a complete being could pull something like that off. And that spirit is incomplete. For a revenant, it's darn good. I'll admit it. Maybe ... ninety percent of the man is reflected in that echo. But that's still ten percent shy. And as time passes, the spirit will reflect less and less of the man he was."

They looked at each other in one of their silent conversations.

"Considering you didn't even want me going upstairs," I said, "I presumed you preferred me to let him get on with his work, rather than helping him move on."

"Feels like the least we can do for him," Connie said.

"Well, if you change your mind, I'll be happy to come back and help him move on."

"What about the furnace?" Connie's mother asked.

"He broke the bindings so he could dismiss the elementals. They were too powerful. They interfered with his meditations."

"Then what are we supposed to do for heat?"

"He believes that d-grade should not be too powerful for him to account for. But that's up to you. I've bound him from interfering with any elementals or other spirits bound within this house. So you could, if you want, bring in more c-grade elementals and just make him deal with it."

"We won't do that to him," Connie's mother said with a sigh. "We'll make due with d-grade. I suppose."

"And if they're still too much for him?" Connie asked, wincing, as though she didn't really want to ask.

"Best he can do is talk to you about it."

"I suppose that will suffice," Connie's mother muttered.

"Apart from that, I've taken the legal steps required of me to allow him to continue here and pursue his Great Work. Mostly involving making sure he doesn't hurt anyone, and that he'll move on once he finishes."

"But you said he won't finish," Connie said.

"He won't," I said. "But he'll keep trying until he loses cohesion and fades away."

In my opinion, that was a cruel fate. But I appeared to be a minority of one in that room, because the other two looked at peace with that solution.

Weirdos.

Then it was just a question of them signing off on my work, my certifying that the problem had been handled, and their paying me. The usual minutia that invades all forms of business at some point.

Once that was finished, I stepped out into a cold, rainy world.

It didn't feel depressing to me, though. The cold of the breeze. The smell and feel of the driving rain, bringing life all around me.

These were reminders that I was whole, and very much alive.

I took a moment to enjoy the feel of rain on my face, before I got back in my van and left.

SIGN UP FOR STEFON'S NEWSLETTER

Stefon loves to keep in touch with his readers, and loves to keep you reading. The best way for him to do both is for you to sign up for his newsletter.

Sign up at http://www.stefonmears.com/join

If you sign up for Stefon's newsletter, you get...

- Monthly updates about his publishing and travel schedules
- His latest news, in brief, and answers to reader questions
- A free short story for signing up
- List-only offers and occasional specials
- Plus a free short story every month!

ABOUT THE AUTHOR

Stefon Mears wonders what spirits are running around most places. Stefon has more than thirty novels to his credit, and he never stops writing. He earned his M.F.A. in Creative Writing from N.I.L.A., and his B.A. in Religious Studies (double emphasis in Ritual and Mythology) from U.C. Berkeley. He's a lifelong gamer and fantasy fan. Stefon lives in Portland, Oregon, with his wife and three cats.

Look for Stefon online:
www.stefonmears.com
himself@stefonmears.com